Owen,

Dream BIG!

-Abby ♡+

Copyright © 2022 Abby Paine

Illustrated by Henry Littleworth

All rights reserved.

Papa and the World's Largest Meatball

written by Abby Paine
illustrated by Henry Littleworth

for Grandma and Papa

Thank you for allowing me to share your amazing story. You've always shown me that with love and dedication, anything is possible.

—Your granddaughter, Abby

My favorite part of Sundays was calling Grandma, not only to hear her voice but I especially loved telling her about my stories from school.

On the phone, I suggested to Grandma that they do something different today. Papa must have overheard. He shouted from the couch, "After this game, why don't I treat you to dinner at our favorite Italian restaurant, Mulberry Street Trattatoria?" The thought of having a night off from cooking had Grandma jumping with joy.

Unfortunately, every Sunday looked the same for Grandma.

It meant sitting with Papa as he cheered for his favorite football teams.

As Papa devoured the meatballs, he could taste every delicious spice in each bite. He imagined what it would be like to have an endless number of them or even a giant meatball. Suddenly, he had a BIG idea.

Papa couldn't hold in his excitement, telling Grandma about his new project, "I've got it! I'll create the World's Largest Meatball!"

Grandma wasn't surprised this because Papa always time was different. He was of the world's largest meatball. She knew not would believe in Grandma promised Number One and stand by him.

by an idea like
thought BIG. This
aking on a challenge

everyone
her husband, but
to be his
Supporter

The following Sunday, Papa listened to his favorite football games on the radio while he began building the meatball oven.

Just when he felt overwhelmed by how much work was ahead of him, Grandma came outside to cheer him on.

"Papa, you've got this! Good news, all the kids and grandchildren are flying here for this year's festival. I even got us matching outfits!"

Meanwhile, the chef began mixing the ingredients for the BIG recipe.

Of all the projects he'd taken on during his lifetime, Papa was sure this was the most difficult, but **he loved the challenge.**

At last, he finished the custom meatball oven. It was time for cooking!

Once the meat was transfered into the Italian friends began what they called From that moment on, every half recorded and cooking would last until the Italian Fest of meatball supervision, indicating it was fully cooked. world record, the meatball cooked all the way through, the previous record holding oven, Papa and his fellow "meatball monitoring." hour the temperature was the unveiling on Saturday at ival. After four days the oven switch turned off, In order to beat the had to be fully intact, and weigh more than 1,100 POUNDS.

Hundreds of people gathered and enjoyed food vendors at the festival, but Papa could only focus on the meatball. It still needed to be moved on stage by the forklift and then weighed by the Guinness Book of World Record's judge.

The Guinness Book of World Records' judge signaled to Papa it was "go time." We all gathered as the forklift raised the meatball off the ground.

As the machine lifted the meatball to the stage, it wobbled and juices began seeping out of the oven. He needed the meatball to remain undamaged or all of his hard work would be gone. Papa, full of nerves, clenched Grandma's hand and the crowd cheered on as the forklift slowly set the meatball on top of the giant scale.

"Well, looks like this is the moment we've all been waiting for."

The judge looked down at the scale and read aloud a weight of 1,707 pounds, which had never been done before. Papa had created the world's largest meatball!

* * *

The final step to holding the official Guinness World Record was a taste test. This would determine if Papa's oven really cooked the meatball all the way through.

What you see here today is a pretty big meatball. In fact, it is the World's Largest Meatball at a very delicious 1,707 pounds. Congratulations! We all cheered louder than Papa had for any Sunday football game. = He did it!=

CERTIFICATE

The largest meatball was achieved by The Italian-American Club of Hilton Head Island in South Carolina, USA

While everyone dug into eating the meatball, Papa was overcome with gratitude for the support he felt taking on this BIG project.

As I hugged him, he held on to Grandma's hand and said aloud, "If you dream it, you can do it!"

Beth and Joe Carpinteri at the Italian Heritage Festival in Hilton Head on Saturday, November 18, 2017 at the unveiling of the Guinness World Record's Largest Meatball- 1,707 pounds.